P9-DCH-833

For my grandmothers
▨ P. R.

For Paul
▨ D. P.

Text copyright © 1998 by Phyllis Root
Illustrations copyright © 1998 by David Parkins

First edition 1998

Library of Congress Cataloging-in-Publication Data
Root, Phyllis.
Aunt Nancy and Cousin Lazybones / Phyllis Root ; illustrated by
David Parkins.—1st ed.
p.   cm.
Summary: When Cousin Lazybones comes to visit Aunt Nancy but
refuses to help with any of the work around the house, she must
figure out a scheme to get rid of him.
ISBN 1-56402-425-3
[1. Laziness—Fiction.   2. Cousins—Fiction.]   I. Parkins, David,
ill.   II. Title.
PZ7.R6784As   1998
[E]—dc21   97-51157

10 9 8 7 6 5 4 3 2 1

Printed in Italy

This book was typeset in OPTICather.
The pictures were done in oils.

Candlewick Press
2067 Massachusetts Avenue
Cambridge, Massachusetts 02140

AUNT NANCY
AND COUSIN
LAZYBONES

PHYLLIS ROOT

illustrated by DAVID PARKINS

CANDLEWICK PRESS
CAMBRIDGE, MASSACHUSETTS

Aunt Nancy didn't turn any cartwheels when Cousin Lazybones come to visit. She knowed he was so lazy even his shadow didn't get up and follow him around. But he was her fourth cousin three times removed on her great-aunt Hattie's sister's side and family was family, so what could she do?

Ezekiel the cat knowed what to do. When Cousin Lazybones strolled in the door, Ezekiel strolled right on out and hid behind the woodshed. No way was he waiting around to wait on Cousin Lazybones.

"Hope you don't mind some company for a month or two," says Cousin Lazybones. "When do we eat?"

"Soon as you feed the hens and gather me some eggs from the henhouse," says Aunt Nancy. She goes to get him a bucket of chicken feed.

"I'd be purely pleased to help out," says Cousin Lazybones. "But it don't make sense to go looking for eggs when the eggs can come looking for you."

So don't he just start throwing chicken feed on Aunt Nancy's floor and calling out, "Here, chick-chick-chick-chick-chick"?

And don't the chickens just come cackling and clucking through the doorway, chicken fleas, feathers, and all?

"Now, ain't that an idea?" says Aunt Nancy. "Why didn't I think of that? Course, somebody's gonna have to clean up after them chickens, and it can't be me. I got to get lunch on the table."

"Shoo, shoo!" Cousin Lazybones flaps at the chickens. "Reckon I'll go gather the eggs after all. I got to rest up a bit first, though. My knees is wobbly from all this work."

So off Cousin Lazybones heads for Aunt Nancy's rocking chair, and off Aunt Nancy heads to the woodstove to finish the fixings for lunch. Pretty soon Aunt Nancy is knee-deep in work, and Cousin Lazybones is sawing down a whole forest of trees in his sleep.

He does get up long enough to eat seventeen helpings of lunch, howsoever.

"I'd take it kindly if you fetched me some water from the spring for washing up," Aunt Nancy says as she's clearing the table.

"I'd be tickled purple to lend a hand," says Cousin Lazybones. "I'll just take this here bucket and set it right outside the door. Reckon it'll rain before long and fill it up."

"Now, ain't that an idea?" says Aunt
Nancy. "Why didn't I think of that? Course,
if it don't rain by evening, there won't be
any clean pots to cook supper in. I'd go get
the water myself, but I got to be ironing
the bedsheets."

So off Cousin Lazybones goes with the
water bucket. He's near as far as the door
when he hollers, "Ow-w-w-w-w!" and gets
all bent over.

"Just a little hitch in my git-along," he tells
Aunt Nancy. "Right here . . . or maybe here.
I'll fetch the water soon as I rest up a bit."

So off he heads to rest his git-along in the rocking chair and saw down another couple of forests.

He does get up long enough to eat twenty-two helpings of supper, howsoever.

Aunt Nancy's ready for him this time. "Water's already heating on the stove," she says. "I wouldn't mind a hand with the washing up if your git-along's not too hitched."

"I'd be pleased as petunias to help," says Cousin Lazybones. "These here dishes ain't but half dirty. I'll just turn them over so's we can use the other side for breakfast."

"Now, ain't that an idea?" says Aunt Nancy. "Why didn't I think of that? Course, I don't know what we're gonna do when both sides is dirty."

"Reckon then it'll be your turn to wash," says Cousin Lazybones. "Right now I'm plumb wore out from all this thinking. I feel a rest coming on."

And off he heads for Aunt Nancy's rocking chair to clear-cut another couple acres of trees until time for bed.

Now, Aunt Nancy had more brains than God gave a whole flock of geese. She could see the way things was gonna go with Cousin Lazybones around. She knowed who'd be doing all the work and who'd be doing all the resting up.

"Can't turn him out," Aunt Nancy told Ezekiel as she emptied the dishwater behind the woodshed. "Family is family. But enough is enough."

That night Aunt Nancy tidies up so good even a cockroach would starve to death.

And next morning don't she just stay in bed, even when the sun is hanging halfway up the sky?

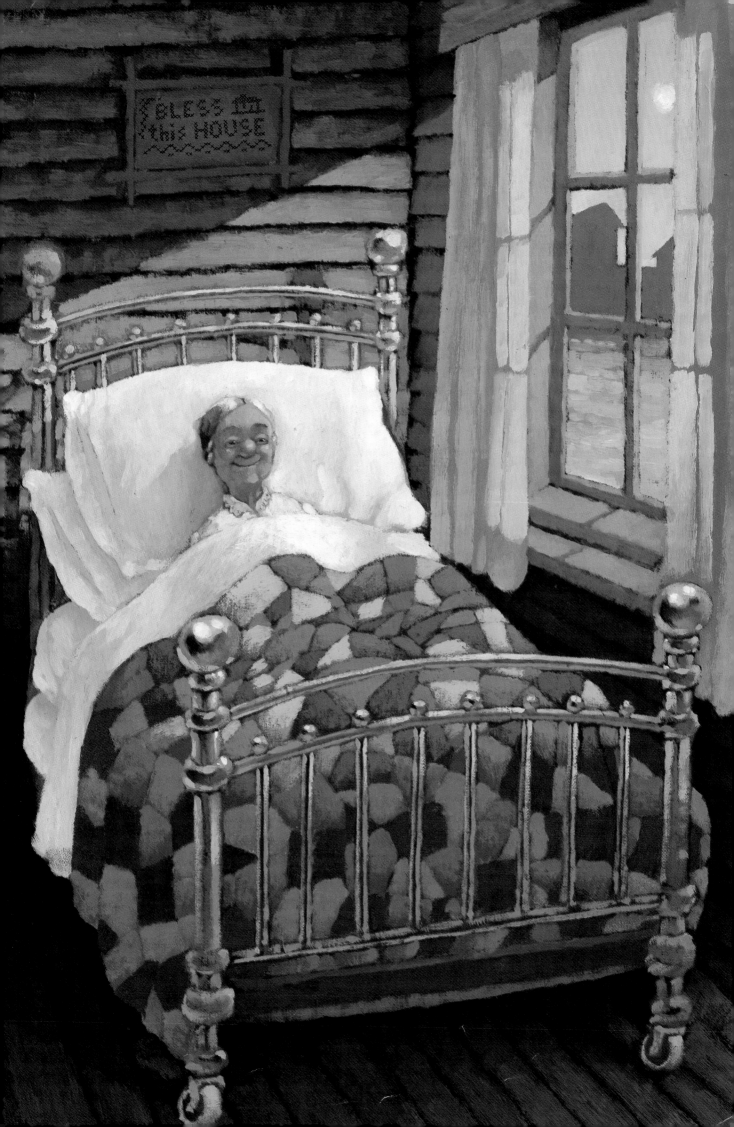

Along about noon Cousin Lazybones rolls out of bed. But the table is as bare as a possum's tail.

"Aunt Nancy?" calls Cousin Lazybones, all pitiful like. "When do we eat?"

Aunt Nancy moans and hobbles to her rocking chair.

"Reckon you'll have to fix yourself something," she groans. "I woke up this morning with a bone in my leg, so's I can hardly walk. Not only that, I got a chest full of breath and such a terrible mess of brains in my head I can't hardly think. This being my spring-cleaning day, it's lucky for me you're here to help, you having two good legs and a head full of good ideas. After you cook and wash up you can sweep the floor and shake out the rugs—"

Cousin Lazybones jumps like a frog in a frying pan. "I just remembered something," he says.

"—and scrub the stove and wash the windows—"

"I think Uncle Wilbur's looking for me to stop in and visit him soon," says Cousin Lazybones.

"—and dust the ceiling and polish the lamp chimney and—"

"Matter of fact, I believe I'm late," says Cousin Lazybones.

He hightails it out the door like a chicken at a fox convention. Aunt Nancy watches him down the road, till he's no bigger than a dust ball.

"Come on out, cat," she calls to Ezekiel, behind the woodshed. "With this bone in my leg and this breath in my chest and all these brains in my head today, I can't think of but one thing to do."

Ezekiel pokes his head out. What does he see but Aunt Nancy whooping and hollering and turning cartwheels all the way around the yard.